MARVEL

MEET FIVE MARVEL SUPER HEROES

MARVEL

Los Angeles • New York

© 2022 MARVEL

This Is Spider-Man © 2021 MARVEL

This Is Ms. Marvel © 2021 MARVEL

This Is Shang-Chi © 2021 MARVEL

This Is The Mighty Thor © 2022 MARVEL

This Is Kate Bishop: Hawkeye © 2021 MARVEL

All rights reserved. Published by Marvel Press, an imprint of Buena Vista Books, Inc. No part of this book may be reproduced or transmitted in any form or by any means, electronic or mechanical, including photocopying, recording, or by any information storage and retrieval system, without written permission from the publisher. For information address Marvel Press, 77 West 66th Street, New York, New York 10023.

SUSTAINABLE
FORESTRY
INITIATIVE
Certified Sourcing
www.sfiprogram.org
SFI-01415

Printed in the United States of America
First Edition, September 2022 10 9 8 7 6 5 4 3 2 1
Library of Congress Control Number: 2021950101
FAC-029261-22217
ISBN: 978-1-368-07367-7

If you purchased this book without a cover, you should be aware that this book is stolen property. It was reported as "unsold and destroyed" to the publisher, and neither the author nor the publisher has received any payment for this "stripped" book.

TABLE OF CONTENTS

World of Reading

LEVEL 1

MARVEL
SPIDER-MAN

THIS IS SPIDER-MAN

Adapted by **Emeli Juhlin**

Illustrated by **Steve Kurth, Mike Huddleston, Geanes Holland, Tomas Montalvo-Lagos, Olga Lepaeva, and Tomasso Moscardini**

Based on the Marvel comic book series **Spider-Man**

MARVEL

Los Angeles
New York

This is Peter Parker.

Peter lives in Queens.
Queens is in
New York City.

Peter lives with his aunt.

Her name is Aunt May.

Peter loves Aunt May
very much.

Peter is in high school.
He goes to Midtown High.

Peter loves math.

He loves science.

Peter works at the *Daily Bugle*.
He takes pictures.

Peter's boss wants pictures of Spider-Man.

But Peter has a secret.

Peter *is* Spider-Man!

He was bitten by a spider.

The spider gave him
super-powers!

Spider-Man can climb walls.

He can shoot webs.

Spider-Man has super-strength.

He also has spider-sense.
It warns him of danger.

Venom is in the city!

Venom is no match
for Spider-Man.

Spider-Man keeps the city safe.

No one at school knows Peter's secret.

Only Peter knows.

Peter Parker is Spider-Man!

THIS IS MS. MARVEL

Adapted by **Emeli Juhlin**
Illustrated by **Devin Taylor and Vita Efremova**
Based on the Marvel comic book character **Ms. Marvel**

Los Angeles
New York

This is Kamala Khan.

Kamala lives in Jersey City.

She lives with her parents and brother.

She has great friends.

Kamala is Muslim.

She is a good student.

She writes stories about
super heroes.
She likes Captain Marvel
the best.

One night, a strange fog rolls into the city.

The fog gives Kamala
super-powers!
She can change how she looks.

Kamala makes her own outfit.
She becomes Ms. Marvel.

Ms. Marvel can grow big
or small.
She can stretch parts of
her body.

She has super-speed.

She has super-strength.

She can heal herself.
But it makes her very tired
and hungry.

Ms. Marvel keeps Jersey City safe.

Sometimes the city is quiet.

Sometimes it needs her help.

Ms. Marvel has to stop the Inventor!

Captain Marvel will help her.

They work together.

They find where the Inventor
is hiding.

Ms. Marvel grows bigger and
bigger!
She is ready.

The Inventor is no match for Ms. Marvel.

Captain Marvel thanks
Ms. Marvel for her hard work.

Ms. Marvel learns a lot from other heroes.
She is proud to be part of a team.

Jersey City needs a hero.

They need her.

Kamala Khan is Ms. Marvel!

MARVEL

SHANG-CHI

THIS IS SHANG-CHI

Adapted by **Matthew K. Manning**
Illustrated by **Steve Kurth and Geanes Holland**
Painted by **Olga Lepaeva**
Based on the Marvel comic book character **Shang-Chi**

MARVEL

Los Angeles
New York

This is Shang-Chi.

Shang-Chi works at a bakery.

He lives in Chinatown
in San Francisco.

But Shang-Chi has a secret.

He is a master of martial arts!

Shang-Chi was raised in China.

His father was named
Zheng Zu.

Zheng Zu taught Shang-Chi
and his sister, Shi-Hua.

But Zheng Zu was a cruel
teacher.
One day, Shi-Hua stood up
to him.

She was sent far away
as punishment.

Shang-Chi missed his sister
every day.
He kept up with his studies
even though he was sad.

Zheng Zu taught five
schools of fighting.
They were each named
after weapons.

The five schools were:
Hand, Hammer, Sabre, Dagger,
and Staff.

Shang-Chi became the champion of the Hand School!

In Russia, Shi-Hua also
became a champion!
She changed her name to
Sister Hammer.

As he grew older, Shang-Chi learned Zheng Zu had a secret, too.

Zheng Zu was an evil sorcerer.
He had plans to take over China,
and then the world!

Shang-Chi fought his father.

And Shang-Chi won!

Shang-Chi now lives
in America.

He became a hero.
He even became an Avenger!

But Sister Hammer has chosen
to be like her father.
She has become a villain.

Shang-Chi will never stop
trying to save his sister.

Because Shang-Chi has
another secret.
True heroes . . .

. . . never give up!

MARVEL

THE MIGHTY
THOR

THIS IS
THE MIGHTY THOR

Adapted by **Emeli Juhlin**

Illustrated by **Devin Taylor and Vita Efremova**

Based on the Marvel comic book character **The Mighty Thor**

MARVEL

Los Angeles
New York

This is Jane Foster.

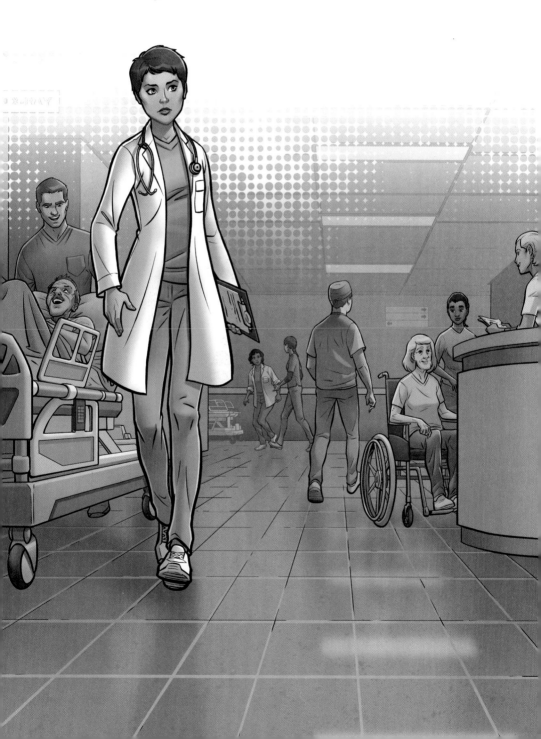

Jane is a doctor.
She helps people.

Jane is sick.

Thor is worried about her.

Jane meets the Avengers.

They also help people.

Thor cannot lift his hammer.

He must fight without it.

Thor's hammer calls to Jane.

She can lift the hammer.

Whosoever holds this hammer, if they be worthy, shall possess the power of . . . **Thor**

The hammer changes Jane.
She becomes The Mighty Thor!

It is what she is meant to do.

Jane is not sick when
she uses the hammer.

The Mighty Thor is very brave.
She uses her powers for good.

She saves lives.
That is important to her.

The Mighty Thor flies fast.

Black Widow caught a thief.

It is Loki!

He fights the
super heroes.

Loki cannot win.

Black Widow and
The Mighty Thor stop him.

The police thank them.

The super heroes saved the day!

The Mighty Thor teams up with
the Avengers.

It is her job to protect people.
It is what she is meant to do.

Jane is The Mighty Thor!

THIS IS KATE BISHOP: HAWKEYE

Adapted by **Megan Logan**

Illustrated by **Steve Kurth, Geanes Holland, and Olga Lepaeva**

Based on the Marvel comic book series **Hawkeye: Kate Bishop**

Los Angeles
New York

This is Kate Bishop.

She is Hawkeye.

Kate lives in Brooklyn.
She loves her part of
New York City.

Kate is friends with Clint Barton.
He is also Hawkeye.

Clint trains with Kate.
They work together.

Kate is skilled
with a bow and arrow.

Kate trains to fight.

She works hard.

She is strong.

Kate is a good teammate.

She doesn't need super-powers
to be a good hero.

She wants to learn everything
she can.

She learns that being a hero . . .

. . . is not always easy.

But every heroic act
is worth the effort.

A hero's work is never done.

Danger can strike at any time.

Kate is ready.

She can handle anything.

Even Tony Stark.

Kate depends on her friends.

And they depend on her.

They can do anything . . .

. . . together.

Kate is learning every day.

She is getting better every day.

Kate Bishop is Hawkeye!